The One Rupee Taker and Other Stories from Nepal
Flash Fiction and Short Stories

Sushant Thapa

Ukiyoto Publishing

All global publishing rights are held by

Ukiyoto Publishing

Published in 2024

Content Copyright © Sushant Thapa

ISBN 9789367954133

All rights reserved.

No part of this publication may be reproduced, transmitted, or stored in a retrieval system, in any form by any means, electronic, mechanical, photocopying, recording or otherwise, without the prior permission of the publisher.

The moral rights of the author have been asserted.

This is a work of fiction. Names, characters, businesses, places, events, locales, and incidents are either the products of the author's imagination or used in a fictitious manner. Any resemblance to actual persons, living or dead, or actual events is purely coincidental.

This book is sold subject to the condition that it shall not by way of trade or otherwise, be lent, resold, hired out or otherwise circulated, without the publisher's prior consent, in any form of binding or cover other than that in which it is published.

www.ukiyoto.com

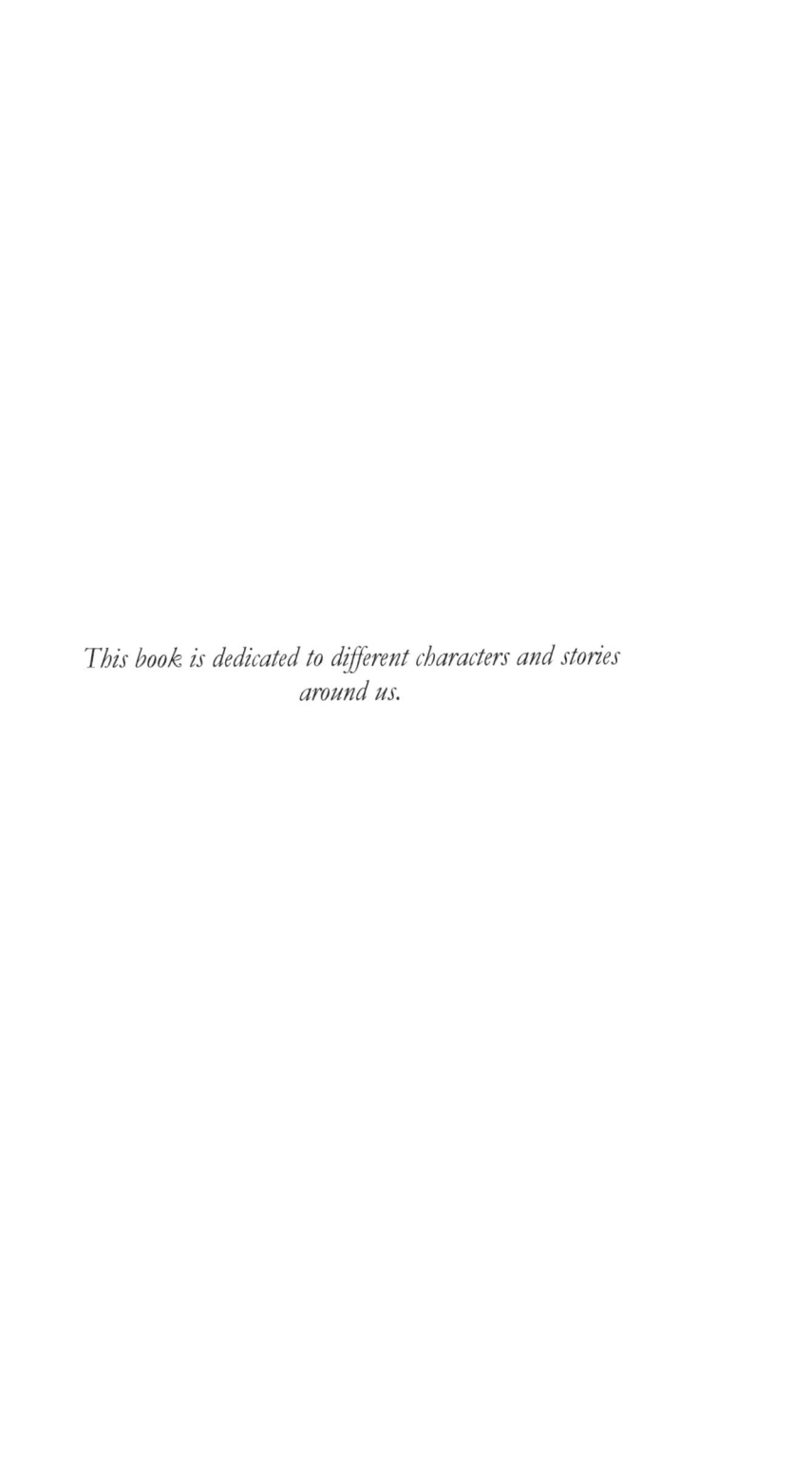

This book is dedicated to different characters and stories around us.

CONTENTS

The Glass Slate	1
Stranger than Fiction	6
Discovery	9
The Guava Tree	13
The One Rupee Taker	15
The Masked Interview	18
An Outlaw Poet	23
Social Media Industry and My City	26
The Wandering Child	30
The Heat	36
Cup of Choice	44
Her kind of love	44
The Rejected Manuscript	48
Fly, Fly, Fly	51
Who is Holy Here?	60
The Beginning Saga	65
A Triangle Love Story	70
Vincent's Blog	78
The Shadow Within	83
The Window of a Freaking Mind	86
The End	89
Knockings on the Door	93
About the Author	*98*

The Glass Slate

Recently, Fai had got more interested in her studies. She was a loner. Her mother used to do daily chores for neighbours against a sum of money. Her father had a small shop that sold second hand goods and Knick-knacks that he got from the dealer—some of them were antiques—more like trinkets. The merchandise in his shop fascinated Fai.

Her father narrated to her stories about these strange objects. He unraveled the mysteries of the town and wove stories around them to try and sell the objects to his clients. The dealer provided him with goods sold in auctions by museums and by abandoned high schools and tour groups. Rusty sleeping bags, mountaineering gears and all kinds of skiing stick—even golf clubs, a tiara discarded by someone who did not understand its value—such merchandise were the focal points of his stories.

Her father kissed her on her forehead and told her a story every night before she went to sleep. These stories were woven around the objects in his shop. They were not like the story of Big Fish in America. The story of the Big Fish was from the story book she got from the school library. It was a strange tale—the hero's daddy would turn out to be the fish at last which had swallowed the ring of hero's mommy. The library at Fai's school would only allow them to borrow one book for the weekend.

The whole family shared a black and white television set. It was on television that she saw the American shops for the first time. They sold many fanciful items from toys to lovely dresses to cars and more. It was America that dominated her thoughts while she lived in the hills of Nepal. America seemed very picturesque and she pined to visit the country.

It was December. In the hills, it was smoldering cold. It felt as if something was buried in the hearts of the people living there—very deep—and the coldness of that thing was making them numb.

Now, she was old enough to read and write. Her classroom was on the second floor of the school. It was near the balcony. Besides, her class, there was a standard two classroom. It belonged to the primary section of the school. The children in the primary only got to listen to and recite rhymes from books. She fancied teaching numbers or numerical counting to those little children. The school was not a well-to-do one. It lacked in certain basic infrastructures like copies and books. A black slate was provided only to those who were in secondary level, like herself.

The primary class had pictures of Santa, rocking horses and marionettes that fascinated her. To her it seemed that the Santa was running away with the huge sack of goodies. In her imagination she flung opened that sack belonging to Santa and lined the toys in her father's shop where he would be ready to make stories about the objects from the rucksack.

Her father had told her the story of a pair of big boots in his shop. The young cobbler loved them and did not want to return the repaired boots to the owner. The owner in any case had discarded them as he bought a pair of shiny boots. The cobbler had sewed them, mended them and polished them till they shone like mirrors. The cobbler lived in the little town. He looked after his sick mother and was able to afford her medical bills with the money he earned from mending shoes. The boots and the cobbler ultimately parted when he needed more money for her treatment.

Her daddy would tell her stories about golf clubs. One of them was so close to its master, he claimed that it swayed and surfed in the air like anything to maintain the projectile of the hit. The golf club would feel where its master was aiming and send the ball to the right hole. It would not let its master down. She had asked, "Daddy, how did the golf club know what the master thought?"

Her daddy would always answer, "Look little Fai, we need to empathize and feel at one with the objects so that they can hear our heart beat too. This will kindle a heart in them as well".

One day Fai had a story to tell. She said, "Daddy I want to tell you a secret, I have a glass slate where I write. I found it in the basement of your shop."

"Oh, tell me little Fai, how will the letters be visible on the transparent glass slate?"

"I write not only letters daddy but numbers too. They are visible to me. In my heart they have kindled the fire of closeness—I write them from my heart on the glass slate, with an ink-less marker, usually. I can write as much I want, and the marker would never be empty or out of ink and neither will the glass slate be inked or filled with the numbers. I project table of mathematics onto them daddy."

Little Fai's daddy was surprised! He said, "Little Fai, you have grown up now and have woven your own story. It is your very own story dearer and closer to your heart and you have found the first object that inspired you, fueled your imagination."

Little Fai cherished her father's words. But, why did her father look concerned? Little Fai could sense that in her father's face. She asked "What is it, Daddy? I see that you are worried."

Her daddy could not reply to the child. He recalled something that he had seen when he had gone to take some goods for his shop from the dealer, who was richer than him. The dealer's daughter who was only about three years old went to the nearby Montessori. Fai's father had thought that children were only fond of stories and that they only played. But he had seen the small girl write on a slate made out of glass. She wrote with a washable marker and she was narrating something to her father eagerly. The small child seemed so excited and happy.

Fai's father was looking at the glass slate on which his daughter was pretending to write. He could sense from the movement of her hands, that it was some letters.

"Invisible letters," he thought. "I will make them visible."

He realized that he could do something so that his daughter could write clearly and enjoy reading and writing.

He found a big piece of rectangular plywood in his storeroom. He had some white paints. Last time, when the carpenter had come to attach new doors and windows to his small house, he had left behind a piece of ply as it was in excess.

"I will paint it and provide my daughter a real marker with black ink this time," he said. He prepared the board and stuck it to the glass slate. He bought Fai a marker. Fai was very happy. Every night when he narrated stories, she would tell him more stories that she thought up as she drew and wrote on her glass slate with her real marker, wiped and rewrote. Fai excelled at school and dreamt of bringing education to the little town. Life began in the hills.

Stranger than Fiction

Old Mr. Bubble sat in his armchair and observed the passers-by. The city rose in the morning when the clock struck five. The silence gave way to morning sounds.

Women walked and talked on the footpaths about educating their daughters and little sons. They believed every lesson should not be taught more than forty-five minutes. The leader's inability to rule the country became a conscience of some new job holders. The morning walk seemed to be all about venting such problems.

The road ran across the suburban sight. No cargo trucks were parked in the morning although, the day ran on wheels. The path was spacious, and the children played without being deterred. The road carried buses, vans, and students cycling to school amidst flocks of sheep that strayed into the road as they grazed along the greenery that often lined the edges or some abandoned patch of grass under the supervision of shepherds.

The city felt like it had to be observed more closely and that is where characters like Mr. Bubble stepped in. Mr. Bubble was a high school teacher. He lost his son during the civil war period in the army. His son's memories haunted him and every day he washed the memories with a heavy heart. Every evening Mr. Bubble took a walk on the highway. He had lost spaces in his life. Now he seemed to be filling merely a vacuum. The lack of action in his life made him realize the pauses. Fishes do not think of dying when they are safe inside the water. Mr. Bubble was in his bubble and he was still safe until things started getting out of his hands like the time when his son died. He couldn't stop his son from dying and that did him no good.

One evening while he was on his regular jaunt, he discovered a grassland beside the highway. There was a small pond which did not look dry although, the water was slightly muddy. The trees seemed to bear fruit and some looked burnt. The grass seemed to be smeared with chemicals so that they could not grow. If the place was meant to be abandoned why bother spreading chemicals on the grass so that they would not grow? Mr. Bubble was already inside that grassland and away from the road.

The evening sun was on its way to the dark land somewhere behind the moon. It was about to hide itself and let one part of the world be steeped in darkness. The sun knew when to get hot or when to get cold. Mr. Bubble thought that the world was a fabulous discovery till it was over-used by all.

One thing that Mr. Bubble pondered was why houses seemed deserted in the grassland? Perhaps nature took matter into its own hands when things were not cared for by humans, this was a fact and not fiction. Fiction, after all, had been manmade although it could contain natural ingredients. How we perceive every other reality can contain details like clockwork as even things have their hours, minutes and seconds that keep ticking. A beating heart has always been a clockwork before it could be forgotten for good.

Mr. Bubble was really alone after losing his son. When the closest people walk away or disappear, we really cannot make friends with inanimate things. There can always be a reality which engulfs the truth which is stranger than fiction.

A lonely house and again a vast grassland where wind blew alone without a purpose, the sight of an old man and somewhere far, how tides hit the beaches lining the ocean went unnoticed.

Mr. Bubble just waited for another day and another lonely walk away from people's sight, but he wasn't running away from himself. Old age was a thing that one could not run away from because death came slowly—speed was only for the escapists. Those who have the time to wait do not worry about the passage of hours, minutes and days…

Discovery

Ray copied all the questions from the question paper and looked out of the window. Twenty minutes had passed, and he wasn't able to answer any question. Mathematics had always been very difficult for him. He always failed in mathematics but passed other subjects. He managed to get promoted to higher classes. He had reached the highest class of school with the lowest grade in mathematics.

"What do you expect out of me?" he would question his mother in an arrogant manner.

"Why don't you study mathematics during your exams?" his mother would ask.

"Even if I study it, I wouldn't make it," he would reply, and scribble poetry.

He had a diary in which he wrote poems. On top of every poem, he would write proverbs, and those proverbs related to his poetry. Writing poems was the only virtue he was gifted with. He wasn't good at sports either. During the whole duration of a game of football, he would not get a chance to touch the ball — leave alone to kick it.

Ray would question his existence in his poems. He would lament about his life, the life which he had not seen nor lived. He created mountains of words and he lived his life vicariously through his poetry. The thought of writing poems made him feel alive.

Many times in the examination hall he would scribble poetry in rough sheets. His class teacher who was also the examiner was aware that Ray could only copy questions in mathematics but solving them correctly was another matter. He was not the only one who was weak in mathematics; there were many of them in his group. But he was the only one who wrote poetry, and that made all the difference.

Ray would try to solve the questions in mathematics, but his answers never matched with the answers at the back of his book.

Poetry was his only hope.

How fragile his life was without it? Reflections in poetry were like life itself. Poetry could reflect happiness, pain and illusion in life. Mathematics was very abstract for him. The answers never matched and sometimes he doubted the questions too.

On the other hand, poetry also questioned his existence, but always provided him with answers. It made him think and ponder upon the questions of life. And the best thing about poetry was that answers were different for each person and they need not match and be the same. This openness made all the difference.

Ray was finding answers to life in poetry and the answers were his own. The answers did not need to match with the answers in the books. It was unlike the mathematics they taught in school in every sense.

Poetry could be contemplative in nature but mathematics in school was derivative in nature— derived from facts and laws in form of numbers. However, while trying to solve math problems, he glimpsed poetry could be like mathematics and only the ways of finding or reaching conclusions were different. He felt mathematics and poetry were two different paths to examine life and to prove that life exists. The process and methods might be different, but the conclusion was always similar. Both the subjects had a similar derivative – to explain life around us.

He even felt that zero, the smallest number in mathematics could also be meaningful. Zero was capable of having meaning on its own – it could mean nothingness. Yet, when combined with other numbers it could still be meaningful. Similarly, in poetry words were capable of providing infinitesimal meaning when they were on their own but when combined with other words, they could provide infinite meanings.

Mathematics explained the laws of universe in numbers and poetry explained it in words. Mathematics could elaborate a new dimension of time and space. Poetry could also elaborate a new dimension of time, thoughts and space. Senses could be unbound with words and with numbers too.

Mathematics surpassed time in its calculation and poetry was immortal in words. Mathematics could calculate in numbers the wholeness of the universe: poetry could describe the idea of the universe in words. Mathematics helped to create inventions with precision: poetry also invents with words – with brevity and precision.

Ray was only trying to solve the equation of life and draw conclusions in his own way. He felt and saw the subtle differences in both the subjects and yet both had some strains of similarity.

Poetry had brought him to limelight in his class and in school. Since he was good at poetry his teacher felt the urge to help him with his mathematics. He was the same examiner who always noticed Ray while he copied questions in the examination hall.

Ray had begun by copying questions of mathematics, but eventually he was all set to find his answers too. It took him time to find his answers through numbers, but eventually he succeeded to pass his mathematics exam of tenth grade. The difference worked out pretty well for him.

Ultimately, Ray realized the difference between poetry and mathematics. The difference which he realized brought different modes from life together and produced a meaningful ending for him. His teacher read few lines of poetry from Ray's diary to the class:

For, what is it that Poetry can do?

It can make tremble a single leaf of a tree among many, and make you its master

It can let you climb on clouds while you are on the ground and are finding your stand

When your heart aches and you find pain in others

When you stumble and see others falling too ….

The Guava Tree

The guava tree always stood in seclusion. The lemon tree also grew beside it. The potential of the lemon tree was curbed by the sharpness of its thorns. Jubilant children did not care about thorns on the lemon tree and swung beside it on the guava tree where their swing was attached. The potential of children was one thing and that of a tree with respect to its thorn was another. Ah! The sharpening of the senses and the sharpening of thorns, two things related in Nature, but created differently by Nature for two different subjects. Still, children cherished the playful act of swinging from a tree.

The tree that stood in seclusion was not at all alone because children visited it regularly. Had the children not cared to visit the tree, it would have remained alone. The thorny tree was also not lonely because it stood beside the guava tree and children visited the guava tree as their swing was attached to it. Every day they visited the guava tree after school. It was their place of recreation. They embraced the joy present in the air around the tree. The tree welcomed them with its spaciousness. The lemon tree was the only thing that occupied space and interfered with the space for children to play. The children were not able to climb or swing on it because of its thorns.

The children visited the guava tree every day after four in the afternoon. Manu was among those youngsters.

He was a shy lad. He didn't talk much in school. He occupied small space in the library while he visited, and sat with his books. Ideas and words went above his head. He sat with his vacant mind in the vastness of the library. His mind dwelt around the guava tree and its spaciousness which was very lively for him in comparison to the sedate, quiet library. He liked the vastness and liveliness around the guava tree.

Manu dwelt happily on the secluded space of the orchard where those trees stood. Sometimes, he used to swing alone at the fall of dusk. He found himself even in the aloofness. The tree caught and captured his scattered self and he always felt himself to be slightly amassed when he was near it. Loneliness did not occupy any space near those trees, especially near the guava tree. Manu did not feel vacant at all; such was the ambience and the feeling, the feeling of personal space, in the vastness of nature. His heart and mind were occupied in that playful act of swinging on a tree. The freshness of the air and invigorating atmosphere made him feel lively. He did not feel alone. He was present in the wholeness of the space. He kept swinging on the guava tree beside the lemon tree, without caring about thorns of the lemon tree.

Eventually, he was able to make few friends. His shyness gave way while he played. After all, life in the orchard was not bad at all. Even beside the thorny lemon tree, goodness prevailed. Yes, the guava tree always stood there in its seclusion like in the beginning of the story.

The One Rupee Taker

Every day he visits my home and takes only a one-rupee coin. Not more and not less. If I try to give him a two-rupee coin, he asks, "Do you want me to take this coin?" and he won't take it. He is in the habit of taking a one-rupee coin from my home and perhaps many other homes. I can only see him coming to my home to take a coin. I do not care if he visits other homes and collects coins, for I care about his visit to my home because of his regular habits.

We see him in gatherings and ceremonies at other places. He sits flat on the ground. They serve him well in many social functions. Unconcerned, he sits politely and leaves in a well-mannered way. Yet, his daily habit of taking a one-rupee coin from my home worries me.

"How very forgetful of him!" says my dad if he is late.

His tension is unlike that of a housemaid who lights a single cigarette in the afternoon after finishing her morning chores. A single cigarette puts the maid to relief. But a single coin puts the man to unrest every day.

People say he is loosely wired. Decades have passed. But he has not changed his habit. Everybody in the town has ceased to talk about him now. They are not worried about his activities. He is dressed untidily in dirty clothes often. He is well built, stout and tall. He seems to come from a healthy family. The only thing that concerns him is the daily collection a one-rupee coin from every home. He might have hoarded a vast amount by now.

He used to talk to my grandfather in those days when I was young. He would see my grandfather having lunch at the dinner table through the window, and he'd say, "Well, you are having your lunch, should I not be having my coin?" I used to be young but now I can write his story. I'm a grown-up man now, and I can write things about the one-rupee man.

Many times, I have placed a coin in front of the man myself. I would place it on the windowsill, he would murmur something, and I would say—"It's there." Silently, he would feel the coin with his hand and take it. He would say nothing to me.

Once, my little niece gave him a two-rupee coin. The man asked my dad, "Why do you create such confusion? Why do you give me two rupees instead of one?"

Once a day, we see him standing in front of the window of my house, but he is very careful not to visit more than once a day. Perhaps it bothers him, and that's why he is particular about it.

Some say he was a rich businessman, and that his business partners deceived him and he lost every penny he invested. He got detached from the business world, but he does collect a one-rupee coin from everyone. He continued to have a relationship with the monetary world in as much that he would have his daily dole of a one rupee coin. He makes sure that he comes to collect a one rupee coin from us, and we get bothered about handing him his single one-rupee coin. The give and take process dilutes the tension. Yet, it seems to be a never-ending process that holds the burden for both parties.

The Masked Interview

Checking vacancies every day in newspapers; Mohan had developed a habit of applying whatever position suits his academic qualification. Like the turning of an age a new beginning was touching him. This was the third place where he was applying within a period of one month.

"Character is an outfit," was written on the poster hung on the organization where Mohan was applying for the job. Somewhere in the organizational structure a future of character was taking shape for Mohan. This was like an anticipated journey.

Mohan noticed that people were accustomed to believe in a condition that reading is just another condition. Even someone who reads a hoarding board is considered too rigid. Why read everything so much is the question deep rooted in every house.

Mohan was a media reader, he used to read latest updates and he cherished books as well. He knew that books have pages that do not talk unless a will is casted to turn the pages. Mohan was interested in non-fiction these days, it somehow made him calm and non-fiction did not sound that personal.

"Isn't the ultimate purpose to write is to find hope?" Mohan silently made a belief and turned the page of the book that he was reading.

An interview was awaiting Mohan. It was getting closer each day. It was waiting to showcase the certificates; a treasure to be revealed. With a high focus on microscopic vision wider skills get developed. The not so academic world can teach an academic from day to day events. Marx had asked: Who will educate the educators?—the answer is society although; it might be too apparent. Mohan was also in a country that had thousands of lessons to teach and multitudes who dare to learn those lessons and that gradually moved the society. There was a heritage city that worshipped living goddess. The goddess was named 'Kumari' – a child. Mohan remembered that lots of seats in the airport lobby were occupied by tourists in his country. There was no gunpowder in the air, instead peace wafted like air.

To put every effort and sit in a chair facing the questions hurled at him made Mohan thoughtful. His heart knew the nervousness. He was inside a business organization that was looking for a communication officer. Mohan had a degree in mass communication. A masked clerk guided Mohan to the interview room. The sanitizer at the entrance of the interview was also saying something about the era of the interview. There were masked and unmasked interviewers. Looking at them anybody would say that there is a difference in unmasking and masking; the psychology that accepts or negates such things.

Mohan read about a forest fire that burned animals and herbs in the forest. To read about the fire felt time consuming and time did no justice to those burnt things. Furthermore, police brutality, natural calamities and terrorists capturing and ruling a country—such was the feeling of a masked world. That world cannot be free even without the mask that shields the virus. Who gets called for interview in that world is itself a question climbing the peak of time.

"Necessity kills passion" an art corner of a national daily made headline. While preparing for the interview Mohan read it with a doubt. He was nervous when words from that headline traveled inside his mind to the interview hall. Mohan felt that to live without analyzing is to forsake the meaning and no absurdity is brilliance. Mohan decided to speak without hesitation in the interview; whatever he felt important to share.

Earning to live came like a necessity to Mohan. Having a talent and to sale it obviously felt different than window shopping. There are individual passions which can be like a wisdom stone, but it comes with a responsibility to sustain and make it workable for life. This is a chapter of reality from the book of life. Yet a verse has to be contributed; a verse that alleviates and adds to the beauty of life.

That interview room had a globe and a map of the world on the wall. To be in that room was to share the world. To convince and influence the interviewers with answers was like adding a flower to the world.

"Give a short introduction about yourself," the first interviewer asked Mohan. The interviewers were spread in a circle on the luxury sofa in that room.

The question seemed to be the hardest to answer. Can qualifications introduce a man? This question immediately knocked his heart although he answered that question briefly including the qualifications. The answer was accepted.

"Do you have work experiences with any media?" the next interviewer posed the question about the experience.

Mohan conveyed that he had worked for a media company as a communication officer.

"Why did you leave your previous job?" another question came from one of the interviewers.

"I had to leave the city where I was working due to the pandemic. I have come here to stay with my family," Mohan answered.

We see that you have mediocre qualifications although, you meet our requirements. Can you show us something extra?" This question came from another interviewer who was watching Mohan from the corner of the room.

Mohan showed his certificates about the workshop that he had attended outside the country. The workshops were of international standards and also relevant to the organization.

"We will get back to you soon," said the last interviewer.

The interview was short, but Mohan left with what he could recollect. He later realized that he had forgotten to remove a mask of corona from his face that day. The interviewers were not able to see his face, but he had eye contact and he answered every interviewer sitting in that room.

Mohan came back to his home. The realization about the masked interview was brewing in his mind when he took a shower. That memory was being washed by water. He had read about Spanish Flu and the devastation in the history of mankind. Mohan felt light after he had spoken for the interview. This time his qualification and skills matched with what the organization was looking for. He was ready to travel for the work of communication officer and that was also a plus point for the organization. He turned his television on and the news about the pandemic was streaming on the screen. Mohan did not feel like applying for another job although he saw some relevant vacancies in newspapers. Mohan decided to wait for the call from the organization. The pandemic age was dropping its tears but there were smiles on the faces of candidates who were called for the interview that day and hope was beaming everywhere.

An Outlaw Poet

"An Outlaw Poet" was written in front of Mr. Karki's house. This was the sign on the entrance gate of the house. The hedges separated the house from the road. An old yellow light was shining in the evening. The house gate might have been golden in color, but it looked yellow with age. Binod was cycling when the day was beginning to close its chapter. The highway ran down to the gate of Mr. Karki—the outlaw poet.

Beginning to arrange his papers, the poet spread loose words—a first step into the outlaw journey was to recollect the lost heart. "Magnificent" was the word that he wrote, just to cover up the old wound. The poet could not move from the fact that his old crush had only asked him where he was, but she had no intentions to love him back. They were in a different city now for years.

"A Poet with a lost heart need not skip a beat." He tried to console himself.

The poet moved on in his life and he had nearly forgotten about the woman that he loved. It was one-sided although the time he spent with her in the college was one of the best experiences to him. They were together in a college internship. Imagination being a tool of the poets for ages could not materialize the love. A lonely imagination had triggered a rebellious romantic poet. Beauty flowed from a hurt heart, the heart which bore the figment of imagination.

Why do you have to be a romantic talking about birds, colors, butterflies and skies when you own a forgotten heart?

What flowed like stream and was beauty for the world, was a statue of realization that could crack any moment.

A wooden heart is another thing born out of carpentry in an outlaw poetic garage. The carpentry takes place in a garage jangling with sharp iron tools. The tools are alone although they fit somehow to change the shapes of the wood. Likewise, words tone a poet, they are alive and so is a poet. The alphabets are the tools; mind is a cutting machine—sharp and breaking the useless memories into pieces.

Mr. Karki had reached his point in writing poems where he felt satisfied. Whatever happened with that woman did not disturb him. She had reached him on social media, and they acted like friends. Mr. Karki however had no intentions to go after the woman. He was happy with his life.

That evening Binod never knew why it was written in front of Mr. Karki's home—An Outlaw Poet.

The rain making music, cracks on the ceiling, taste of thunder and the sound of the typewriter were so evident. The definition of being an outlaw had to be scripted. Poetry did not use polished sentences like prose and that was what Mr. Karki loved. The house which he lived in was an old generational house. It came with little tax to the government and huge compound. It felt like living in a suburb, with all the comfort. It was all about laying back and living in the world. Mr. Karki was well connected with writing peers and that was enough for him. Somehow the suburb like feeling called for distraction from stardom, for better.

Mr. Karki's poetry was well received in the international community as his publication rate was high. Maybe he would be discovered by society soon. Mr. Karki published through self-publication but all of his poems were accepted by quality literary magazines that cared about the forbidden path of poetry. Mr. Karki did not want to wait for independent publishing houses, he did not bother writing a synopsis to the independent publishing houses, but Mr. Karki believed in quality works and that is why most of his poems were accepted by literary magazines. Mr. Karki was learning to edit and wait, he thought to approach traditional publishing houses. He read about the story writers that one should sustain 100 rejections in a year. Maybe that is what being an outlaw meant among all the illegal definitions that have chances to appear and get defined by others.

Social Media Industry and My City

The bus was traveling in a common route to the capital city. The capital of the country matters to most. Many kinds of industries function from the capital. The film industry, the publishing industry, also the education industry. The flight of labor is also one of the industries which take manpower from here and sales them abroad. The business of toil has completely been a legal matter. It feeds kids here, sends them off to school, runs a house and the wives can proudly flaunt their jewelries in their parties. The perfect world gets mirrored here in the age of plastic attachments. Relationships that corrode inside the crimson walls of the city's happiness are never scripted and popularized.

Home or away for people; every city has its own stories. The relationships in the country breathe in the foreign air and cross the real flights of agony with a heavy heart—I mean the journey of a real flight on a plane which bears the agony of leaving the beloved in the home country. Pain in the mirror is not real, but fiction is. Fiction in its essence establishes many notions which can be applied to real-life equations. It is a draft of long-distance findings, figureable and touched in proximity to behavior expressed in the paper which may be unique and unanticipated. Only a revealing quality can share the feelings. Only expression is the gateway to new ideas of the mind. We have many stories that remain untold and unwritten due to fear of unacceptance.

So, the bus has started and I am amused with these thoughts in my mind. I won't say I am preoccupied with these ideas. I am on an easy roll and I watch the wheels go round. A habitual truth speaker may think low but is never out of content. He won't entice you and arrest you with his words, he is as free as breathable air even when he is with you during the conversation.

Even social media is a new industry now like the film industry. We can call it the social media industry. There are many actors in this social media industry. Every person using social media is a social media industry actor. The industry was down for some time technically this week and it immediately gained attention. I am not living in the capital although I can observe the day-to-day events of many successful social media actors from the capital city in the social media industry. They are more than social media industry actors; they are not mannequins clothed like a human but real-life character although their presence is only on the screen for me till now. In social media, they have supported me with my writings. On a positive note, this is the need of time, how everyone needs social media and capital adherence with cities. Be it the place, power or connectivity. I can write about the capital city from here, I wonder what I could have written about this place (my hometown Biratnagar) from the capital city (Kathmandu).

It is night now and the bus has stopped for dinner at a local eatery. I am writing my diary regularly. I do not write for fame, tonight it seems I will write to get a good sleep. I have never written for fame, and writing comes spontaneously and I have to say that I do not have a reason to write. I am drawn to it and poetry. I feel if I only write prose I will lose that essence of literal words and brevity with a quality of alleviation which verses contain. I am writing this diary entry and this is a blend of fiction and reality. If you feel like I am lying think that is the fictional part. "Fiction is a lie that speaks the truth" is a famous saying which fits this situation. This bus journey is a lie but the vehicle which these words harbor and move is the reality. Language is an art and the essence of it is a day-to-day struggle to not drown in the sea of art but make meanings that calm the low-spirited.

Suburbs and outskirts of a city have always been my kind of thing. I can lie back and observe the whole world. The main city and the market are always at my reach. My city is under rapid urbanization. Its face has drastically changed. There is a world that breathes here. Nothing is too separated. I feel this city has everything for everyone. There are bars, shining colorful lights, the laughter of youths, college goers' sentiments of education, and verbal expectations in the streets when they return from their long lectures in the late afternoon. The rich sweat trickling in the gymnasium, dreams crushed for someone living in the streets although he is bold in physique. I have not seen people living on the streets in my city. Maybe I have traveled less at night. I do not know which face the city hides on the streets at night.

The Wandering Child

After long hours in class, Saroj yawned and his world could be seen in his wide opened mouth; like lord Krishna who opened his wide mouth containing the universe, the galaxies and planets.

Even things like eating in class and dreaming in the day was his pastime. Belly full of comestibles and mind full of questions were his forte. Just like the galaxies and the moving planet earth, his mind revolved with questions about music, culture, politics and history. Literature too was his subject of interest.

Teachers in school never gave much attention to what he thought outside of the syllabus. Saroj would question everything and he would do what he wanted with his time at home, even during his study. Tasting chapattis filled with rice and fresh chutneys was how he would savor the boredom in class.

During his study time, he enjoyed stories and someday he wanted to write like great writers do. He wanted a leisure life, filled with books. He wondered if he can spend life reading and get paid for it.

Saroj filled his mind with good things. He listened more and spoke less. He was always attentive to changes around him. Politics drove him mad sometimes. He analyzed that people always blamed governments for the lack of things. He sensed that changes should come from an individual and their deeds.

He believed in luck, but he worshipped work. He believed in god, but he valued human consciousness. Greater than god, the common good was what he would want to partake in. Religion divided mankind, he thought. But he believed in the faith of the spirit.

One day as he was reading poetry beside his window, he saw a small child who seemed alone on the road. The child was carrying a book in his hand, and he seemed lost in the vastness of the city.

Lots of people came and went on the road, but they never stopped by to talk to the child. It seemed people lacked the motive or the reason to talk to the child

The child had dark curly hair, a fair complexion, bright blue eyes and a good physique. Yet, the child seemed to be too silent.

Perhaps he had no stories to tell, but if Saroj could get stories out of the child—he assumed it to be more interesting than the stories in the book which the child carried.

It was a story book; Saroj saw it from his window. The book was very colorful and it caught his eye. Two things were colorful as he noticed—they were colorful and unusual. It was the blue color of the child's eye and the colorful book.

As Saroj went near to the child, the child looked up to him and seemed very blank in his expressions. It seemed there arose a vast confluence of questions in the child's mind—the child seemed little agitated and nervous.

Saroj had gone out; climbing down the staircase and taking a turn down the shutters of shops. The child immediately felt Saroj approaching. He was standing in the sun, and wanted a shade. However, he seemed nervous as Saroj was approaching near. Therefore, Saroj did not approach the child directly.

Saroj stopped by a shop nearby and bought a packet of Bonbon biscuit for the child. The child was sitting under the shade beside the stairs leading to Saroj's residence. Saroj also bought for himself another packet of the same biscuit. Saroj assumed that the child wanted some love and someone to hear his story.

He handed the biscuit to the child and the child took it without hesitation. Maybe it was the hunger rumbling in him.

"You can keep the packet," Saroj said lovingly to the child.

The child smiled at him and erased the sweat from his forehead. The shade had given him a good shelter. The child had begun to eat the biscuit like anything. Saroj also ordered a fruit juice for the child and handed it to him.

"What is your name brother?"

"Where have you come from?"

"My name is Sakar; I have come from the hills of Hile."

"Why are you alone?"

"With whom have you descended down?"

"I came down by myself; I want to go to school," The child answered.

"The earthquake broke down my school last year, since then we haven't been receiving proper education," The child broke with ease.

In the plains of Tarai region earthquake did not cause much damage last year. Saroj remembered his school which was functioning well; this was his last year in school.

He would finish his 10th grade and would apply for college in the city where he was living. That was his plan. The child had descended to the city from the hill for good education. It was so easy for Saroj to carry out his plan, but the child had to carry such a huge step leaving his family and travelling all alone. Still, good education was not easy to be received because the child was all alone.

The colorful book was his English book and it had all the good stories. The child was carrying a 2nd grade book. Saroj assumed him to be of 2nd grade, but later on he remembered that since last year there was no proper school in the hills of Hile and the child should get admitted to 3rd grade.

The evening had dropped its curtain already and it was dark. Saroj thought to make some preparations so that the child can stay with him.

Saroj was also alone as his mother had gone to her paternal home. Saroj lived with his mother. His dad gave his life for the service during the civil war. Saroj knew the hardship of providing education to the child and efforts which parents have to bear. The bearing of a child and making him a grown-up requires huge incessant efforts.

When every little demands of the child has to be fulfilled and every little moments of betterment expected; parents have some hopes from the child too.

Parents wanted to see their child growing successfully in school and in life. His single mother invested all her time and efforts in his schooling in school and outside school—in life.

His mother still had hopes and expectations from him. And for Saroj nobody understood the struggle better than his mother because she was all alone from the beginning of time, he was a little kid when his father left the world.

"Sakar has to be taken back to his home," Thought Saroj.

"His parents must be worried," Saroj said to the shopkeeper who stood nearby.

The shopkeeper told Saroj that he had heard the news on the radio regarding the lost child named Sakar.

Sakar took the child back to his parents that evening in the local bus.

Saroj wrote letter to the District Administration Office of the region of Hile that evening after handing Sakar to his parents.

Sakar's parents offered shelter to Saroj that evening although they were poor. They shared a common meal.

Saroj missed his dad, but it felt like he would forever remember this affection and warmth which Sakar's family exhibited to guests.

The letter contained issues of education and opening of schools after earthquake.

The Heat

Being a celebrity had not been easy for Kartik. The action movie director had called him over dinner at his place. Kartik's recent wedding with an actress had blown enough air for the public. The private affair took a turn—it was no longer private. Perhaps the cost of stardom was to lose inner peace. One of Kartik's fans had committed suicide because Kartik had turned him away from interview at his home. Kartik had been a reserved kind of celebrity. He abstained from meeting people for interviews while he was at home. He was so busy with his character roles that he hardly saw beyond the hovering clouds of acting. Kartik memorized his dialogue before his driver drove him to the film set. The movie was named "The Heat." It was an action movie, but there was a club dance scene. Some drunken sensibility was to be carefully unfolded. The only fear that Kartik had was one. What if he forgot to act? What would he do? After his dad left the company which he co-founded nobody contacted him from the company.

His driver used to say: "*Sahib*, all movies have one thing in common—they are all *kissas* (famous stories) like talk of the town, or *guff*." Kartik laughed and told the driver to focus on the wheels. Kartik said, "You better tell those *kissas* to *Buhari*, I am sure she'd find it entertaining. Also, bring her and your little daughter to the movie set sometimes." Before being a driver, the man used to work as a make-up artist in Mumbai. He had seen the silver shining glassy images of Bollywood. It was all like a glassy world, shiny and filled with pizzazz. The glassy world hid its fragility.

"Not mixing profession and passion S*ahib*. What if she leaves me and runs away with the hero?" —the driver said jokingly as he parked his car. They sat under the gazebo in the garden; this was where the fight scene was about to be shot. This was a spacious setting; already the crowd had gathered to see one glance of the hero.

The director came from a theatrical background. He had started his acting career from a very young age. Dramatization was a skill, which came from the English bard himself—the director believed. The director believed in the dramatic power of written words. He wanted to capture that energy and depict it on screen. With an ever-ready producer who was a poet—the direction was going smooth. The conglomerate of professions and thinkers, were carving the masonry of the movie. The management part was good, but the director had some trouble with the dialogues in the script.

"I need a responsible writer," the director said to Kartik.

"Unedited scripts with longer dialogues ruin the feeling in actors," the director expressed his concern.

"It takes a whole lot of energy and ploughing of the mind, to make a movie," said the director.

Kartik said, "It is not a business, but a show of creativity."

"I do not want to lose the dramatic art factor and visual cinematics," the director added.

The director had hired Ranjit to write the story, but Ranjit wanted to act. He would secretly ask the make-up artist to put make-up on his face. He would recite the dialogues from the script that he wrote. He did this behind the curtain of the make-up room. He'd hide the script in his belly; inside his shirt. Ranjit focused too much on this acting behind the curtain. He threw tantrums on the set. He was less concerned with writing a fine line. He grew impatient every minute. He'd yell at the make-up artist for not cleaning the mirror in the make-up room properly. He'd recite his dialogues in disguise, in front of that mirror.

The director wanted to add a historical war scene in the casting as a tribute to the Late King Prithvi Narayan Shah. From flying cars in movies to thrilling effects, the director wanted to shift his camera. Ranjit was asked to collect and research on historical facts, but he was too busy in his own disguise. The love of acting was consuming him. The director knew about it. He had also called Ranjit for dinner at his home and Kartik was also there with his newly wed actress wife. The director's wife was a fashion designer and she also designed wedding outfits. Kartik's wife Komal and Mala, the director's wife, were busy looking at new designs.

The dinner was turning out to be a light evening soirée. The men had pertinent issues to discuss. For Ranjit it was a matter of job. He knew he could be fired from the job anytime. He wanted to talk to the director and replace the hero. This was a tough thing to talk about.

The temptation and heat ate Ranjit from inside. He knew the director was a tough man, with his own rules and behavior of strict adherences. Ranjit was searching for a loose time to initiate a friendly talk with the director. He obviously did not want to talk in the tight presence of Kartik.

Ranjit did not know why Kartik was there. Kartik was already signed in for the movie and had airs of stardom around him. Ranjit wanted to climb up the stairs of stardom. On the other hand, Kartik wanted to climb down the same stairs, after what happened with that fan whom he had ignored for the interview. The director still wanted Kartik to be in the industry till the end.

"Did you see the crowd of public that day while shooting the action scene?" the director said to Kartik.

Ranjit was jealous when he heard the director say so. Before Kartik could reply to the director Ranjit interfered. He abruptly said, "The public disturbed the peace, it affected the boldness of the dialogue—the script demanded something else."

"Ranjit, why don't you work better on the historical facts for the casting?" the director said.

"The heat of the present time demands history to be clear," the director further added.

Ranjit replied, "I think they are older things, what connotations they have now?"

The director said, "That is what you are unable to see, Ranjit. Open your eyes."

Ranjit got irritated, he was realizing something which he should not have. He grew anxious, each moment. How was he to tell the director that he wants to replace the hero, just because he liked acting? The weight of this thought was too heavy on him. He wanted to get it off his chest. Should he talk with Kartik directly and sort out? Kartik was sitting in front of him during dinner. The director had a newspaper under his plate on the dining table, it had the news on the first page. The newspaper carried the news about the suicide of the movie fan which directly and indirectly involved Kartik. Kartik was taken to the custody for the inquiry, the previous day. Kartik told the police that there was no personal envy between him and the fan, and he had not seen the fan before. Kartik clearly mentioned that he never anticipated the mishap. He kept it before the police that he had casually told the fan to ward off citing family reasons.

"The suicide seems like a publicity stunt now," Ranjit said to Kartik in the dining hall.

"I do not understand, who is benefited by this stunt?" Kartik questioned.

"This is totally unexpected, why take a liking for some actor so seriously?" Ranjit said.

"This event has disturbed me a lot, I feel like giving up on acting," Kartik told Ranjit.

"What do you plan to do, sir?" Ranjit asked Kartik.

"I used to be often worried about that. I have no clue till now," Kartik confessed.

"I have to seek my old acquaintances, people with whom my dad spent his official time with," Kartik further added.

"There are some letters which my dad always pestered me to read, he said they were from friendly acquaintances, which I believe were official," Kartik elaborated the expression to Ranjit.

"What can be the secrets in those letters?" Ranjit got curious.

The director bid farewell to both the men. Ranjit was still supposed to work on the dialogues and historical facts and Kartik was to carry his acting career with equal ease as before. The director had asked Kartik to not be despondent with the media and all the news on hype.

That evening after reaching his home from the director, Kartik called Ranjit to his residence. Together they were set to find the secrets in those letters. Kartik found the letters in his dad's study room. The room was kept in the most exact manner when his dad used it during the later days of his life. His dad used to spend his sick days reading and writing in that study room. Kartik never knew at that time why his dad was always busy in the study room.

Now, while he entered the room and switched on the light, he vividly remembered his dad sitting on the chair near the window in that room. His dad used to stretch his arthritic legs on a stool and sit on the chair. Mostly, he used to write. Also official papers would be strewn on his table. Kartik recalled some of the official characters in that room. Lawyers in dark suits and white-collar people always sauntered in and out from that room.

Suddenly the telephone rang in the room, before Kartik could read any letter. Kartik was surprised. Nobody had called his dad's room for quite a long time after his dad's departure. The man who called asked Kartik to sit down on a chair, and relax. The man was about to reveal something amazingly shocking.

Kartik was told that: "You are the sole heir of the company which your dad had co-founded before his death."

Kartik replied, "I barely know about the company. Who am I speaking to?"

"I am the partner of your dad, in the company. I am leaving for America, and I do not have anyone whom I can ask to be the heir. I want you to take the responsibility of a three hundred million rupees company," The man replied.

"Come and meet me in the office, and we will do the formalities," The man said.

Kartik noted down the address.

Kartik looked at Ranjit. Ranjit had told Kartik about his interest in acting before they entered that room. Kartik felt happy that he got a chance to take up his dad's company. He felt glad that he would be near to his dad, even after his death.

Kartik thanked the man on the line, and hung up the phone. He turned to have a talk with Ranjit who wanted to become an actor. Kartik decided to call the director after a while and climb down the flights of stardom. Ranjit knew that he himself was perfect for the role, and now he did not have to hide and act in front of a make-up room mirror. The director believed their consolation in the end.

Cup of Choice

Her kind of love (Subpart I)

"Answering your own door makes you feel low," said Kabita.

Kabi had no reply to those answer-like questions. Feeling of leaving her on her own was like letting a beautiful flower make its presence for some more mornings before the neighbours would pluck it. Many such mornings she became herself; like a flower of color blooming for the day. Kabi was a man of night. His clock ticked his time in a publication department during the night shift in Putalisadak, Kathmandu. Kabita uttered without hesitation in the house. The roof that they shared was their catalyst that helped them with their chemistry to solve their equation of life. Thoughts would hang as sticky notes in their refrigerator, but they would share the night coffee together. When they had travelled to the Annapurna base camp after the marriage they were like two question marks, answering every step of the journey. In the picture they also looked like a dot in the blanket of the snow covering all the shyness. Opening up to each other was like a shaft of sunlight breaking through the window. Kabita always cherished little things. Every day they spoke about the morning and the day throughout the night. Sleep would cherish their dreams.

Setting out and getting things right was always like the philosophical morning or philosophical night and the philosophical sun or the philosophical moon. Life had meanings which helped people speak their mind. But only speaking for the sake of meaning was not what Kabita wanted. Kabita was an interior designer. Abstract paintings and old objects were her fancy. Even her paperweight had a sea inside it—the sea had its own stars. Twinkling stars above the ceiling and scent of fresh paint in the house were her luxury. Caste, creed and diversity of life became the plunge for the sake of painting the world with her eyes.

This was the first year of marriage which was going okay although they were falling apart physically. The physical attachment was turning out to be only platonic.

Could life be led without the art of the bodies?

Can the love sustain without being under the blanket of the skin?

Designing the pause seemed like an eternity that sleeps every night alone. We see the sun every day, but can we care to understand it without the night?

Kabita was a courageous woman. She wanted to be an artist.

"Live like a legend and die like an artist" was what she stood for.

The inability of her husband to penetrate was nothing to her. She was still content with what they had. Her interior was strong, she could design it anyway. Society thought a tough road obstructed their journey. She knew it was a two-edged sword to smile and cry inside the heart. Kabita felt she was lucky in what life turned out for her. She could design walls and her living with Kabi was like a wall of sky showing its stars and its own sun.

They made a journey to the sea in Goa. Goa was filled with lovers, but unlike them. They were named like a rising verse. Kabita meant a poem, and Kabi meant a poet. Kabi could always carve a kabita out of her. He was trying his best to be a poet for her. Time was so real for them. The sudden realization of what trap they were in could not be erased. They were what they had become. It was inescapable. Acceptance and creation were driving them throughout the days.

When Kabita stood as a bride, she posed delicately for the picture. There were flashlights, cameras and the stage was set high. Kabi and Kabita both were unknown to the cursed inability which caged Kabi only later. The dream of being a mother was falling apart for her. This could be the end of everything, but this end had not yet begun.

"Rainbow in the dark is impossible," said Kabi.

"Sky in the dark is a vision," consoled Kabita.

"If Hope is a thing with feathers it must also settle down. Perhaps it seeks a gentle ground."

These thoughts made Kabita wonder.

Adopting a baby is what they were looking for. Acceptance already made them strong. The root cause of the problem in Kabi was yet to be figured out. Some medical sites read that psychological problems could be associated with it. Soldiers were affected with this disability after the war. Rush of modern life did not have time to read about these issues from the newspaper of differences. Queer issue is always talked about, but this remained a personal issue which affected the mode of life. Life is not only penetration; there are other playful acts in the act of sex. Like art movies, watched only by a few people. Liberation comes from the mind of a yogi and also from the mind of the *bhogi*. In the end where you employ the mind is the main concern. Lives matter and mind matters too.

The Rejected Manuscript (Subpart II)

Turning the last light off Kabi was about to leave from his desk at the publication department. Kabi was a stout man, he was not too dark and not too light. He had dark color when he was worn out and his color was light when he was not busy. He seemed to have the look of a well-fed middle-class man. Nutrition made his face red. Kabi was a poetry and fiction editor of the English publication house named "Prism Publication" located in the book hub of Nepal - Putalisadak, where many book shops and publication houses had emerged over the time. One story that striked him in an old manuscript read odd. It was odd because it was only even for him. That story was unpublished by the previous editor; it was rejected by the Prism Publication.

Every night Kabi became a prisoner of the book. He would stay awake in the press at night beyond his regular hours and read the book. Sometimes he had to sneak in the publication house late.

The rejected manuscript looked like a golden *khajana* although it was dusty. Actually, the golden dust made it look like the gem of a pirate. The font in it looked like the letters in some cowboy online magazine; to be specific: The Beatnik Cowboy Magazine. The manuscript was hundred pages in length. The manuscript sounded too literal. Kabi read the first few pages. Kabi felt that we in the society tend to speak for our meanings; people hated the truth and anything literal. Literal things were mistaken for inexperienced blithe—carefree and unnecessarily self-contained and self-satisfied (this was how society perceived). Kabi, was diagnosed with a sexual dysfunctional problem. Only nature could heal it. He was healing slowly, but that was too literal.

To Kabi's surprise the sub-plot in the manuscript read about a man who had the same problem like Kabi, but the man chooses to stay unmarried. There, Kabi felt the crack in the pot. The world broke down for him, reading between the lines. Kabi has found his Kabita, but this particular story in the manuscript got trampled before it stood. Kabi kept on reading the story, but he was surprised that the man was still cherishing life. Saints talked about being alone, Einstein talked about being alone, Bukowski talks about being alone and every creature stands the taste of time in their lives. Social media showcases many balloons of happiness—people rising, people living, and people content with the show. What lies below the plank of happiness is the sprouting reality growing somewhere.

The manuscript carried the individualism and a way of living of a particular man, alone and taking bold steps. The man was a writer who lost his way in himself. This might sound too obvious like the passing time. The man sitting in front of a typewriter the whole day and selling what got inked, travelling alone and losing his heart beside the mad waterfall. Will you believe me if I say the heart can never be insane? A broken body can have a beautiful heart. Perhaps life is an art of the heart when the body goes numb. Sometimes, we should let the world answer our questions.

A question like a child and an answer like a humanitarian formed the basis for freedom in the manuscript. The title page of the manuscript was torn and it did not exist now. To Kabi it felt that the publication house wiped it. But he wondered how come the manuscript was still on the shelf while others went down to the bin. Some hesitancy got reflected here. It could have been printed; it means it is a hidden gem under the sea.

Fly, Fly, Fly (Subpart III)

Music wafted like air in the speaker just beside the wooden ashtray. The bar grew dim. A deer horn hung below the cracked ceiling, an old clock with a wooden brown frame stroked midnight. Few pages were left unseen from the fashion magazine. The table was covered with the flower sheets; the flowers only seemed to be waking in the colorful sedate bar. The doctor had forgotten his stethoscope back at home. Vidya told him he doesn't need a stethoscope and that psychiatrists don't need to pretend that way in front of the patients. It was a disguise, which doctor Khan was using to divert his mind. A unique therapy it was; it helped him when his patients were lying and waiting for him to listen to it all. It was a therapy for the doctor himself; something was secretly building a wooden heart in him through all the carpentry.

Doctor Khan's clinic was opposite to the place where Kabi worked. The night shift kept both of the men alive. For Doctor Khan the night clinic was a choice because it was his personal space, he could have shined in the clinic during the day.

Mental health issues became a theme for Kabita's office where she worked. They were voluntarily working to raise awareness and were also contributing to the green planet. Their designs were in tune with nature and were getting eco-friendlier. The model for the environment which Kabita's organization followed was from the Terai region. The saplings of plants and funds were sent from the Terai region. Biratnagar, the city from the eastern part of the country, was the new hub of green Terai. It also contributed to the environment of far-western region; many villages in the Terai were facilitated and Kathmandu valley also could not remain untouched from it.

The funds were generated even from prisons. The prisoners crafted bamboo and rubber stools and they were allowed to sell it. The funding flowed from the cells and crossed the bars. Plantation works were carried out by the office of interior designing, they were hoping to form a bureau in the eastern part of Nepal— the Terai especially. The valley office was making plans to plant trees also in the hilly region of Nepal, but excessive rain caused floods in the hilly region and houses were getting swept, people were drowning in the rain water. The bureau was made to wait by the floods. Kabita worked day and night to design eco-friendly wall plaster. There would be mornings when she would skip her morning walk, and would design in her laptop.

The marriage which was falling apart was flying from her memory. Only strains of anxiety took hold of her, but she was drenched in the purpose of her flair. It seemed like coming out of the marriage debate which was burgeoning in her head. To remain single must have been just like the man in the hidden manuscript which kept Kabi busy. Maybe this was the other side of the tunnel or maybe the darkness of the journey. How positivity was seeping, how the cracked pot was healing. Only the gold had to be found, just like the Japanese way of mending the broken pot with gold—Kintsugi.

The yellow despair waited to turn golden although, yellow and golden might mean the same. The healing got lost in the process. Mankind forgets that the attire of the body can sometimes be hung in the hanger or kept for drying in the shade or sun. Feelings merge mind and heart; one might not really come to understand if it is the heart or mind that does the feeling. Freedom is liberation from both maybe, but it needs to be felt and not caged.

It showed a talking tree, leaves still minding their own business. The recycle green logo, a paintbrush and natural colors were dropping on the screen. The video was for the advertisement and there were no flesh and blood characters. Animation did the standardization for now.

Like the bubbling imaginative cloud hovering above her the green earth rolled below her feet; cartoonist world unboxing the squares and circles. The rolling circles danced like disco balls, whirling like the heavy waterfall into the river that made her forget the turbulence in her heart. The talking tree and the cartoon for the advertisement were somehow like the falling rain, spattering and reaching the closed window of her heart. There will be grief, there will be pain. Talking and seeing truly will cut like a knife. Seeing is different than looking. No spectacle is needed for seeing. Perhaps loneliness will mask itself and reappear someday. Uncovering that mask of loneliness will be like finding flowers of love in the mud of mind. It will be like sunshine again for one more day.

"I am broke, but I am not a mirror. I am broke, but I am not a crack in the pot. Only vessels crack, earth has its digging."

This line read from the page of the manuscript which Kabi had brought home. It had been underlined carefully even in the manuscript.

"Who drew that line at the bottom of the sentence?" a thought spoke in Kabi's head. This was the first door of a mystery that was closed. His thinking was louder than the silence in the empty room and the thought sounded like a dialogue in the one-act play.

Like a magical plant that emits light and pulls you closer to it like a magnet, the book became an addiction that would not leave Kabi alone. There are some things that are luminous when they are hidden. The book contained hidden words, and those words were not accepted yet they had to be spoken. It seemed that the book found Kabi and only Kabi could understand this choice.

You don't get to read about failures in love when love is only romanticized. A broken heart is not read and felt. Silence is often misunderstood although it has no meaning; such is the ironical receptive capacity of humans. Only the chosen ones find meaning in silence; it is also a life. Virginia Wolf said that she would want to talk about silence in her novel, the thing that people won't say and here Kabi had chosen to read characters silenced for life because they talk and that's a real choice. This reading is a choice for Kabi, and for

Kabita also there is a choice. A choice of never being able to become a mother was ripping her apart. Sometimes, choice is only a truth that needs to be admitted.

Kabita can find a different Kabi and become a mother, but this was not what she wanted somewhere. Maybe she is still not clear and something pulls her close to Kabi. Perhaps it is the pain which has a capacity to attract two lost souls. The job of interior designer was teaching empathy to Kabita and she had begun to understand what pain is. Pain seemed different than failure to her. Pain becomes integral, it is so real. Mental health issues and serving nature by planting trees was moving her. If the world itself needs to be fixed, we are only mere humans. Maybe she saw worth in fixing the world rather than fixing her marriage.

People can get busy with a lot of things. Life tastes different for different people. Barricaded compounds and stationed homes will not understand the taste of travel. Travelers won't understand the inner sheltered comfort of a home. Both are necessary to live a complete life. A complete whole can be made from broken pieces. Healing takes time and a positive attitude. Healing is a success. Fragments come and take space for a long time in life. It takes only a mindset to defeat the opponent of life.

Dr. Khan's clinic got weary in its interior. Patients came and before leaving they complained about the interior. Dr. Khan wanted a peaceful green color which matched with the park opposite to his clinic. Some designs that matched with the green would be perfectly okay for him. Vidya and Dr. Khan got married when they were in the university. They had moved to Kathmandu from New Delhi and Dr. Khan settled for the clinic. Vidya was a beautician. She did a short course in hairdressing, makeup and mehndi art back at a university in Delhi; that was when they met. Vidya originally belonged from Kathmandu.

Kabita and her team were designing for the "Nature Park" which was opposite to Dr. Khan's clinic. Vidya often went there for jogging in the evening. Vidya saw that painting on the wall and fencing was going on in the Nature Park. Kabita and her team were also doing forestation and also the virtual statue model had already been created. The team was observing and demarcating the area to be covered by plantation. Artists would soon begin their ground work. The park office was changing its interior. Vidya came to know about it since the team of artists and designers talked about it in the park office and Vidya also saw that the stonework for erecting the statue had begun. The team seemed fully prepared.

Vidya went back that evening; she narrated the events at the park to Dr. Khan. Dr. Khan promised to visit the park the next day and approach the team of artists for designing the interior of his clinic.

Dr. Khan began his evening in the clinic that night as usual; he was brewing green tea which he prepared for himself. Dostoyevsky's Crime and Punishment flipped its pages on his table. Being a psychiatrist, he loved how Dostoyevsky portrayed the psychology of Raskolnikov; only psychological justice had been done but morally the crime that Raskolnikov committed is a terrible thing to do and living with it must be difficult.

It had to be confessed, it could not be kept as a secret. Raskolnikov says in the book that he has murdered a useless thing and not a woman. Dr. Khan could not stop thinking about how crime can be justified. He kept the book aside.

From the night hour that stood still, flowers in vases lined up near the windowsill were breathing. There was a knock on the door. The clock showed 11 pm. Dr. Khan was greeted by a heavy man, who had a goatee and shoulder length curly hair. The man was handsome despite his heavy attire. He still had the dark glasses against the night hour which was in full swing. It had started to rain. The rain caused doubts in Dr. Khan's mind. He thought about the person who had stepped inside his clinic.

"Was the person hiding from the rain and taking shelter in his clinic?" The thought took hold of the doubtful doctor.

The man passed an old prescription to the doctor.

"He is a real patient; not a trespasser," the doctor assured his over-thinking mind.

The doctor started to turn the pages of the prescription. The prescription was clearly old and the pages were yellow. The prescription had a date which was five years older. Medicines were prescribed to the man.

"I am still in need of the medicine," uttered the man.

Dr. Khan looked at him and the prescription.

"We have to undergo some preliminary requirements for the medicine," the doctor informed the man.

"The prescription says it all," said the man.

"You will feel all right after my little inquiry," the doctor tried to empathize.

"I will ask you a few questions, and then we should be okay"

"Sure," the man agreed.

"What is it that you are curing?" doctor began to ask his question

"This sounds philosophical, but I can tell you that the medicine cures mood," the man replied with some hesitancy.

It seemed that with all the efforts of clearing his mind, the man was able to utter those words as an answer which he was also seeking.

The man looked at the picture frame hung on the wall of the clinic. There it was written:

>Today I am reaching
>
>Tomorrow I shall arrive.

After reading those words the man felt a little free.

The man immediately said, "I undergo auditory hallucination. I feel that people always talk about me. I can always hear them talking about me."

"Is that what you are curing?" the doctor asked.

"Yes, that is what the medicine cures," the man reiterated.

"Over the years I have managed to decrease the dose of the medicine, and I take less mg of the medicine now," the man recalled and expressed to the doctor.

"It is the ladder of success that you have climbed onto," said the doctor.

"Do you see the difference?"

"I think a lesser dose will be enough to help," the man remarked.

"Figure it out what purpose you seek with life," another remark passed from the doctor.

"Die with passion, live like life isn't a reaction," this line came to the man's mind.

Yes, life needn't be a reaction to every other thing. Legends take a firm path and stick to it. If not, do what is right and needs to be done. Live a legacy and be part of it. The world will follow or time will recognize you. An overbearing is not being responsible. There will be pauses in musings and there will also be exclamations in life. Pauses are not always silent.

The manuscript of the man drew the attention of the entire publishing house. This time for real.

Who is Holy Here?

Before switching on the light of his home for the evening Sagar always stood for a while. He was considered somewhat unholy and switching the light on for the evening was always regarded as a sacred affair. Pauses in the evening also start like the morning sun that boils and spills itself above the hill in the horizon—the pauses rise, they get detached and tangled with contradictions. The neighbourhood woman always passed her unholy comment about the light of the evening whenever Sagar would switch it on. She would say: PRAYERS FIRST.

The woman was holy. Her home had a temple like steeple structure, trident and the large orange colored wavering flag. You know when people renounce living, when they even leave their husband and family and live as a saint. Somehow people are capable of changing like that. The woman did not want Sagar to turn on the light bulb of evening in his home which she believed was holy. The holiness imposed on the light was supposed to be sacred like the light emitting, absorbing, reflecting sun and the moon and nobody was allowed to touch the light without being holy or saying their prayers.

Sagar would dwell in the grassy front yard of his residence. He read Whitman and also had an American taste in music. He had some illness in his throat which made him the silent observer of the town. He could not talk for longer hours. He could have joined teaching but the doctor had advised him to talk less. Ramesh had been his classmate in college. Sagar had always been receptive, but was reserved more often. Ramesh was exactly opposite. Ramesh was extrovert and Sagar never thought about such kind of vocabularies which came direct from the books like Word Power Made Easy. These personality traits were like disguises that clouded peoples' habits and bended those habits and fixated a dead end. Ramesh was surprised when he learned from Sagar about this holiness of the light. The neighbourhood woman came as an element of shock—a foreign and strange air blew and mixed with the neighborhood.

Sagar and Ramesh were preparing for their civil service examinations. They needed light in their room and there was a power outage. Now there was darkness everywhere and the neighbourhood was not visible and there was no trace of the neighbourhood woman. Here, in the night something similar was rising in the traits of these two students. It was fear thumping like a silent explosion—only nobody heard anything. The initial days of the examinations had been transparent like an ice cube, now its chill was felt. Sagar began working on his introvert ideal even while preparing for the civil service exams. He was reading a British Novel and was amazed how the vocabulary was gripping and new. Although Sagar was not fan of the British accent in movies his American conviction opened doors and shaked hands with his British oeuvre now. Ramesh on the other hand gathered the lightest bag-pack to hit the road—he was planning to materialize that after the very last evening of their exam. Sagar was still standing like a statue in the middle of his room and freezing with unknown fear. The image of the neighborhood lady disturbed his ears—powerful and strange was that moment which could ferment the image into the sound. That trident, the orange colored flag and the snakes coiling in his dreams all flashed in the darkness that evening. Except for crickets ringing in their ears, every moment was asleep.

A drunkard man was leaning against the mound near the temple like house of the neighborhood lady. His silvery image in the dark was reflected by the moon light. The man seemed to be chanting some mantras in the darkness which was only faintly heard and thinly seen. The man was accompanied by another man who was smoking a cigarette. They seem to vouch for each other. They were drinking and smoking beside the temple. Sagar was trying to figure out what holy sermons the drunkard was chanting. Lugubrious was not the last word which could describe the scene here. Frank and drunken, loud and bossy—the man swelled his voice. He was humble only later when the cigarette smoker had smoked his last puff and when the last drip of his bottle was gulped. This was happening in the court of the temple.

What was wrong here, drinking in the temple premises or the faith with which the temple was constructed? — the boys were in dilemma. The temple was constructed above the residence.

"No blame on the temple," said Ramesh

"Human error in constructing a holy place and differentiating it from home," Sagar added.

"No demolition of the steeple is needed," Ramesh said.

There was light everywhere after that line was uttered by Ramesh. The drunkard and the cigarette smoker had wiped themselves from the scene in the temple. The neighbourhood woman's house and the temple was lighted with the wire lights which they used during festivals.

Sagar and Ramesh did not feel the need to argue with the woman and construe their ideas with her about lightning the holy light. They felt their heart was also too dark, and they got a chance to see what happened in the temple which opened their eyes. The woman was chanting her loud and clear sermons and playing the *Damaru*—she was performing the evening *Aarati* as if things were still really concealed. She was also accompanied by another common devotee. Temple court brings various characters from the society.

The two young boys observing the drunkard in the temple in the dark that is where this story really begins and ends. Realizing that the temple needs offering which demands spill of blood and even butchering of animals is something wrong to think. Not everyone sees the spill of blood and forgets Drunken holy chant of a drunkard is not an essential attribute in plain terms but what the two boys saw that night and realized was worthy. Lights and temples are languages of realization; they only speak with faith. However, the question remains: who is really holy here, the temple builders or the temple goers?

The Beginning Saga

Casually the sun went down. The cool stretch of the late autumn air re-surfaced in what seemed like the seamless evening. Inside an old looking house, Rudra was lying in his bed. There were cobwebs on the walls and ceiling of his room, but the bulb was set very bright. Two steel cupboards full of books and a dressing table covered with a thin white drape was seen in his room. The pillow was set vertically—standing as a backbone of the bed. Anybody lying on his bed was able to taste the level of freedom in that position. Rudra's printer was still on, a poetry manuscript had just been printed. He barely cared about the timing to use these machines. Somebody was about to pay him a visit and monitor his latest literary activities. Rudra got paid for the literary writings which he did all alone. This was the new policy of the government, to self-employ people based on their precepts. One had to remain isolated without family, this was the rule.

The government agent was a skinny man. He had triangle face, microscopic eyes and boastful big-rimmed spectacle and he was spitting the fountain of red *paan*. Climbing the stairs, the man seemed to carefully count the steps as if he chanted a mantra. It was hard to trace any wrong doings from his face. This was one afternoon when the guards did not stand outside Rudra's room. The guards moved around in the initial days, no readers were allowed to visit with immediate feedbacks. Only later Rudra felt that his mind was free.

The literary agent was a potbellied man. He seemed carefree in contrary to the careful government agent. He had fish eyes and long face. He often visited Rudra with the supply of books. The agents appeared within neat intervals of time. The works had to be carried nevertheless. Rudra felt that it was difficult to go on with literary works when no one was watching. The dressing table mirror used to frequently flaunt Rudra's reflection, but it was draped for now. Only print materials surfaced inside the house. After much negotiations non-fictions were allowed.

This time came as a dream to Rudra. People with self-interests had protested the lack of jobs and the time had come. The government had really taken matters into their own hands. Nothing stopped them from capturing people like this—you only had to have talent and no job. The latest poetry collection of Rudra was based on family. He had no idea how the government agents would react to this collection about family. The collection was titled "The Beginning Saga." Somedays felt exhausted, and some were spent in recollections. Every night after writing in his laptop and turning the printer off, he saw the picture of his family. The picture was hidden from everyone. How a picture consoled had been a powerful recollection itself.

"What good is a talent hidden from people?" Rudra had reasoned with Kavya that day. She had to vacate the house for his purpose. She left with tears, asking their teenage son and daughter to accompany her. How were they supposed to live alone? The question did not knock Rudra's mind initially. The draped dressing table with mirror kept haunting Rudra. The family photo was pasted like sticker in one corner of the dressing table mirror. Rudra also had a fine collection of fountain pens. The pens had remained inkless for now, after his family left.

Rudra could shake his memories of being with the family. Once, when an elderly relative of the family had died, large mass of people had gathered in the small house nearby. Kavya spoke of every single known person there with Rudra when they had arrived their home. Kavya noted peculiarities of every single person in that funeral gathering—the color of the short half-pants worn by modern young girls of the family who came from the capital city, the fare charged to them by a local auto, the timing of the sons arriving for the cremation rituals, all were discussed by Kavya in Rudra's family. Well-to-do sons were expected to send money for the cremation rituals, Rudra's wife said, "We will never let such kinds of money shortage for the cremation rituals, our *Babu* and *Bune* would not see us in debt."

The night enveloped its own caricature. Rudra was numbed. He washed his face repeatedly after using the towel each time. He sipped glassful of water, numerous times. His wife used to always ask to rinse that same glass, when he used to drink from it incessantly. She would keep the glass in the kitchen utensil-stand immediately. Now the utensils do not clink without Kavya in the house. Rudra had even started to drink in paper cups. The government agent also spitted his *paan* and drank from the paper cup. Now, they drank coffee in the house. The agent said, "*Bhauju* knew the price of sugar, she had sold us the habit of drinking tea." The agent thought that talking about family would not take Rudra off the track. The agent hit the emotional side, this is how they made writers vulnerable.

Once again Rudra triggered his memory. His wife Kavya had gone to another religious family event, a *sraddha*. Her slipper got exchanged with another woman and that woman followed Kavya to their house barefoot. Along with the slipper Kavya sent snacks in that woman's hand to her family.

Rudra was missing his family, and he had a scorching day ahead. He had taken a matter of translating 500 pages Nepali folk novel to English, he had to complete it in two months. The literary agent had handed thirty-five thousand rupees, and Rudra had accepted the money without being skeptical. Now the only reason to come out of this den was to lure the government agent. If the two agents were to agree, then they could shore Rudra out of this sunken sea of trouble. He missed the desire of the family, there was no solution to it except expressing the grief of being locked up from the world like that.

"You can return the money, but you will lose all your literary affiliations? Is that okay?"

"From now on you can earn by reading, and you cannot write, All right?"

"You will only send book reviews our way, no fictions you can weave," said the agent.

"You will be paid very less, and we cannot guarantee the steady work flow," the agents tabled their view.

"You can live with your family," became the final words. Rudra signed the contract and became a metaphorical reader rather than being a lone writer without family. "The Beginning Saga" went on to win the Kutumba Literary Prize and became critically acclaimed as well as a best seller poetry book. Rudra's family came together after many years of detachment and remained learned forever

A Triangle Love Story

Maybe this is a love story, or is this a story about love? Here love itself is silent. Life for a hostel student in the university was measured in how many loves he could sustain. With no love and with many loves the university had seen Laylas and Majnus committed in Love and committed for love. They gave their life to love. But could never give love to their life. Love was an irresistible desire, to be irresistibly desired. The lovers desired and the desirers loved. In every corridor of the hostel, scripts of love story in pictures were written. In every toilets of the university, the lovers' discourse of desire was painted. In every private ward the lust for reading love's story was celebrated with books of secret love.

For any newcomer the university was like a loveless desire. They somehow desired love but in particular no one loved the idea of love. Some desired love with the rapacious tenacity of desire. They did not care for the lover's discourse and the number of loved ones.

This is a story of Atul. He is a student of English Literature at the University of Kathmandu. He is a loner. Atul had grown up in an academic background. He can only think of falling in love with books. But if he could encounter lovers of the bookish world and go with them into the lover's world he would not step aside. Yes, there was his world and other worlds. He used to wonder about the lovers from Shakespeare's world—Desdemona, Juliet and of course Romeo. He used to think about his future. He wanted to settle down after his studies and get a job of a lecturer and teach about love to his students. He wanted to call them fellow students. He wanted to teach them all he could teach and all he could act to the drama of love. Well, his story hasn't begun yet, his love story.

He wanted to befriend friends and fall in love with them. Seen and unseen lovers or friends could become lovers. He could fancy reading books with them. He had read a story about a necessity of having a girlfriend apart from the male friend. The story was read in the Nepali curriculum of another department. It was more of a feminist reading of the text. Not to be misogynist and to appreciate the feminine in the female.

Atul saw no difference in a friend and a lover, but he was also afraid of the idea to love friends. When asked by a friend about a girl in his class he would say "I do not have such a trend to make her my girlfriend. She looks fine, but I cannot make her my girlfriend." We cannot guess what was in his heart at this moment. Perhaps he thought loving was a dangerous game. He only thought too much in love, but fell less in love. "What about the girl who had inquired about another girl in class? Perhaps it was in trend to ask favor for a friend" he would speak with himself in soliloquy. He felt drawn towards love somehow – he was moved secretly in his heart by this idea of asking favor.

Atul is seen talking over a mobile phone to his lady friend who is not his girlfriend yet. Sometimes while talking he becomes silent and the silence fills his heart. He is talking to her as if she is his girlfriend. Well, can you guess why Atul is silent sometimes? It is love deep in his heart filling the silence. When there comes any discussion over phone about any other person who loved differently than him, he fell silent. He compared himself with that person. This was like an inferiority complex.

Atul felt that the world was large and modern and outside the university in the modern world love can be flashy and colorful, but his love was different and purer in essence. Words won't come out at such times and the silence would raise questions. When the lady friend raised questions about his silence Atul was silent again. It was known to her that the silence and pauses in between the conversation was related to the emotional being of his self. When he got over burdened and serious in feelings words won't come out from his mouth. But he loved the silence because he thought and felt in it and it was his way of loving someone.

This lady friend with whom Atul was talking over phone was sent with a mission. I already stated that a friend asked Atul's opinion about a girl in his class. Atul was unaware in the beginning that the lady friend for whom he used to remain unspoken between the conversations was sent on a mission by a girl who secretly adored him. He only knew it later when conversations progressed. The silences that he felt in conversation over phone made him fall in love with that lady friend. That lady friend was Suman. Suman was sent by Kavya so that she could talk with Atul and convince him and make him fall in Kavya's love. There is also a third friend here – it is Chaya, she is the one who had asked Atul how he found Kavya. Suman started calling Atul over phone and Atul was thunderstruck in his heart with the silences arising inside it. He fell in love with those silences and slowly also with Suman. But it was about time with the silences.

Suman started to dislike his silences utterly. The only reason that Atul loved her was about to be shattered and break like mirror. Suman felt Atul was unreal and was not like other guys and he couldn't love in a modern way. His silence was misinterpreted and taken as a sign of weakness. Did Suman love him? The only reason Atul felt in love with her was already a weakness for Suman. Suman frequently asked him to break the silences and be practical. Maybe she wanted him to talk about all the romances and all the things they would do together outside of the university – in the future. The silence was unimportant now. But the silence came out of the unbearable capacity in the heart, the emotion it was. Practicality of the modern world was way far beyond the walls of the University.

Atul only felt things and considered to establish a connection with things, be it unsaid or unuttered. He found many instances of silences and he loved Suman for that. He could reflect his love for Suman in those silences. Even in the classroom he thought about those silences and how he was lost for words. He couldn't let go of those silences between words. He was bothered by it and if one were to ask him he would have said that he loved Suman because of the silences which he found in their talks. Kavya was also in the same class. Chaya had already told Kavya that Atul did not found Kavya right for being his girlfriend. Kavya was in pain but had understood gradually and had consoled her heart.

Days had passed and Suman started feeling bored with the silences of Atul. After many lectures and classes at the department they began to grumble and the silence was violated at last. Atul was dismayed and irritated by constant nagging of Suman while they talked over phone. Atul often started to feel that he should have accepted Kavya's proposal instead of being attached with Suman. Detachment began to sip in his heart. He longed to detach with Suman. He did not care about silences now. He knew that Kavya had always wanted him. Atul knew that Kavya was not so pretty as compared to Suman but he did not care at the present moment.

Is Atul taking this step out of his love for Kavya? The answer to this question will lead us to know that at last Atul will be alone with both the love gone. The college love was about to be over when Suman knew that Kavya had become Atul's new love or girlfriend. Suman had lied to Kavya that she was doing the job of bringing Kavya and Atul together by becoming a medium and by having conversation with Atul over phone. The story had become different.

What happened was unexpected. Atul had fallen in love with the silences over the phone call and Suman had started to like him too. But that was the thing of the past now. Atul approached Kavya and Kavya had always loved Atul so without thinking twice she accepted his proposal. Kavya was on cloud nine when that night Atul phoned her and said that he loved her. She felt that Suman was successful in bringing them together. Atul began talking over phone with Kavya. Kavya was a day scholar. She was wandering in a village in Kavre one sunny day. Atul was inside the hostel. Kavya wandered in the village just to find a phone booth so that she could connect with Atul. Kavya was very excited and in love with him so she was ready to walk an extra mile just to converse over phone with Atul.

Yes, Kavya comes to know about the relationship between Suman and Atul only when Atul tells Kavya. It happens many lectures later when Kavya was already in love with Atul and had accepted the proposal. Kavya gets angry with Suman and they end their friendship. Suman was supposed to be the medium and she was supposed to make Kavya and Atul fall in love. But Suman herself fell in love with Atul. Even in class they were seen together. Kavya allowed Suman to sit together with Atul although she wished that she was the one who would sit beside Atul. After all Atul was her first crush.

After accepting the proposal of Atul, Kavya comes to know about Suman's and Atul's closeness and their relationship of the past. On the other hand, Suman had been shocked when Atul told her over phone that he accepted Kavya (after many classes, lectures and incidents when Kavya used to kick under the chair where Atul sat. She used to kick right under the seat of the chair. Many such romances happened in class. Kicking the chair might not be romantic, but it was inside the classroom and Atul sat a kick distance away from Kavya. Kavya could reach him that way. Yes, they were ridiculously in love.) Yes, Suman was shocked when Atul himself told her that he approached Kavya and she accepted his proposal.

She was in shock because of the decision of Atul which was very nasty. While they talked over phone in the beginning they used to promise one another that they would never let Kavya know that they were in relationship and were happy, but Atul himself had revealed about his relationship with Suman to Kavya because it was unbearable for him and the past kept coming to his mind. They regarded Kavya as a poor soul in the past. Now, Suman blamed Atul for taking this blunder step. She wondered why he became so insecure.

Kavya was really angry with Atul after she knew that Atul was in relationship with Suman previously. She wanted to leave Atul for that reason and she did leave him later. Many lectures later, it was in the canteen and both girls were found arguing that "I did not get Atul because of you." They blamed each other for whatever happened. Both of them were not in a relationship with Atul now. But they still loved Atul. For Suman it was due to the attachment over phone calls and also the silences of Atul and for Kavya it was due to her liking in the first place (remember she had sent Chaya to ask Atul's opinion regarding herself.) The three of them were devastated due to their love. They even avoided eye contact in the class. Their hearts were battered – only detachment seemed to be the solution for the battered heart. The triangle love could not be sustained anymore by these battered hearts.

Atul now remembers the incident with both of them gone and he feels that it was a mistake and he feels that he has become happy without both of them. Atul began to study as he was always a bookish fellow. The question still remains – "Is this a love story?" Nobody received love in the end. The rope of the love was broken and it did not connect any heart. This was only one incident in the whole university. Many other lovers continued to love in the same way and perhaps also differently. But we only care about this story.

Vincent's Blog

"The pathetic renderings were only what could be written," exclaimed Vincent. He was searching something to write on his blog. He thought of a one-liner or a sentence to start his first and new blog.

"It could have been anything like Vicky or Vinaya or Vinod, but it is going to be Vincent's blog," he wrote on his name bearing and entitled "Vincent's Blog."

"Was it out of sheer will?" he thought.

Seeming to introduce his 'self' and ascribing negation with different names he was nowhere near to stitch the narrative together with what could follow on his blog.

"I will talk about myself, on this Vincent's blog," he reiterated the same thing which he had thought before writing that first sentence. It made him calm.

He felt a draught of wind passing with a swish through his ears. "O, these whispering winds," he exclaimed in all plurality.

"I could have been named anything but Vincent," he said in despair.

"There goes my identity," he spoke to himself.

The unseen plurality of identity was ringing in his ears just like those winds which he assumed to be flowing together, for some reason.

"Maybe this is so wrong to think of," he aired low to himself.

He had noticed the gust of wind to be very noisy.

He had proclaimed in writing—"that gust was noisy, and it was whispering something to me."

"How very eerie," he thought for a while and typed "here goes my writing about these whispering winds."

Vincent closed the window because it was too chilly for him to withstand the wind now. What choices does he have? Do you want him to keep the window open? And withstand the wind with a shawl. It is the first dusk of autumn and Vincent is not ready with a shawl to wrap him up. He was enjoying the wind a little while ago and the wind had whispered something to him as it passed by.

"I only want to take the air and breathe a little, but not these whispering winds for now," Vincent sighed with a relief undertone.

"Just like a silent air, volatile is the name when unuttered," Vincent reiterated about the names which he wrote in the first sentence of his blog.

When we are born and ascribed some name to us, are we not emphasizing with the meaning of the name? We are left with the choices of the name and we choose and make the emphasis livelier by adhering some meaning while choosing. We do not choose names we choose meanings ascribed to it.

"I am uttered as Vincent and not Vinod or Vicky or Vinaya."

"My meaning of the word is attached with Vincent."

"Vincent means 'conquering'." This was his fourth sentence on the blog after that sentence where the whispering winds whispered something in his ears.

His despair with the name was over. Vincent had found and noted his meaning, the meaning of his name that was ascribed to him. The meaning was very particular. He felt glad for a moment and a faint smile in his face was glowing.

He looked jubilant for a while and after some time he got wearied again remembering that the names that have been ascribed with a meaning are not in tandem with the name bearer's knowledge. The name bearer does not know the meaning or the name itself when it was ascribed in the beginning. The name was kept on behalf of the bearer and the bearer would be unaware. The meaning of the name is only known to the bearer if one is curious enough to know it later. The curiosity rose out of life, out of absurdity. There is some search for adherence and fixed meaning in life and also some search in name. Maybe the person can also think about the meaning ascribed to the name and bear the burden of the name through the unknown task assigned to him, after he has known the meaning of his name. How very strange is this? We are called by a particular name and it is related to our identity. Yet, we question, "What's in a name?"

These thoughts worried Vincent and he found no clarity in them.

The whole onymous process was to undergo a change if one were a writer, when literary or pen-names were ascribed by the writers to themselves.

"Are they not ascribing some meaning to themselves too," Vincent thought.

What sort of literary writings would one produce if one believed in some name and the nomenclature of it? Is it related to the literature that they produce or in general to what they do in this world?

"It is all existential," Vincent said to himself at last.

What would his task be? Will it be name keeping or the deeds?

"You have known me by name, you shall know me by deeds" wrote Vincent in his blog.

Those were his final words for Vincent's Blog. Vincent did not want to write about the whispering winds though he believed that those winds whispered something in his ear. He did not want to write about name keeping and pen-names in literature.

"Vincent's Blog" made him think about his deeds. Maybe he will travel somewhere and share his experiences or he will write a poetry. Maybe Vincent will become anything like Vinod, Vicky or Vinaya and again come back to write his blog. Maybe he will conquer himself, rather than 'conquering' others and be better in deeds than he is today. Maybe conquering himself was that unknown task of the name and also its meaning. Maybe he will live his existence and not question it. Maybe he will find the meaning of his name in deeds and not in words and he will willingly pursue his life without chasing names and its meanings.

Just like the carelessly blowing wind, Vincent hoped to do something and set out for life. Maybe he will make his life livelier this way and whisper away his name to the silence of the falling dusk and begin a new dawn for tomorrow and find a new meaning in life apart from his name.

The Shadow Within

Shyam woke up around 12 pm in the afternoon and gazed at his table. His laptop, a capsized half read "Communist Manifesto" and George Orwell's "1984" lay on the table in his room. He had spent the previous night musing in these writings. As a matter of fact, it had been weeks. He also wrote few verses and thought to write some mysterious and yet pervasive prose. Writing was not a problematic affair for him, but the actual time which he was spending on writing was problematic. He was spending a lot of time on it. His friends only chatted or called him on his mobile. He had vanished from every open nooks and corners of the streets in his hometown. He only talked with his family members by going in their room frequently, but he wanted his room all to himself. When his little niece would visit his room to watch cartoon on TV he would feel disturbed. His screen time on laptop was more important to him than the excuse of a child to watch the cartoon.

In the morning Shyam's father would blast the news on TV in his room. Shyam would miss that, utterly. He wanted to be aware of the world, but his timings did not match. The loudspeaker noise from a distant mosque made him open his eyes, this afternoon. In the night he wasn't sleeping, he was thinking and reading and therefore, in the afternoon he was awaking. He was being nocturnal; an owl was his nightingale and he wanted to write like Keats but appreciate the night owl.

It seemed appreciation of an owl in the daylight was not possible.

"These are only day to day issues, and nothing else."

"I have to gain clarity in life, and for that my words have to be clear – I should be focusing on that."

"Every other thing is just an illusion."

Friends would pester him and they would want to know his thoughts on getting married and living a double life. With an empty head he would reply them with a negative nod in gesture and a formal "No" in speech; just to be precise. His friends believed he was becoming only a shadow of the night, and when confronted he would say:

"Shadows at night should never be misunderstood."

"Am I a shadow within me?"

"Isn't shadow something which emerges from within and casts itself outside the body, making a detachment?"

"Well, in the daylight shadows seem to be casted outside, but in the evening they seem to be following us from behind and within."

"There is no escape from the shadow unless we put up the light, and the only thing external than the body is the light."

"Light kills the shadow."

The musings about the shadow had begun to drive him towards light. His friends triggered answers to these questions in his mind. There still was a problem about being visible in the society.

"Being visible in the society only means more light."

He remembered he had read somewhere that "work is freedom."

He felt he knew the insights to gateway of freedom; he was ready for this new chaos within and around him.

The shadow within his self would still be casted, but it would also cast his society along with his dark self.

"That would be the best guidance for me."

"The journey of shadow from inner within to the world outside filled with darkness or light."

The Window of a Freaking Mind

From the freaking window a dead carcass was observed being carried by a mob of vultures. The creaking sound of the crickets in the evening of the dusk vaporized the heat and a slight breeze of the evening air crossed passed through the window. The Jazz was playing in the stereo and a slight blue tinge of the curtain touched the floor. The deer-head with its antler horn was hung in the room above and a brownish leather jacket on the wooden beam reflected the dust on its shoulder. The hat on the wall was round enough to look like a head, which could have been one piece to see, beneath it. Curtain was slightly moved; Peter peeped to his daddy's room. All these descriptions of the room and the objects were in peter's head, just a little while ago when he stood by the window and observed the derailed town. Now, he was inside the curtain and into the room.

There has been enough discussion of the room and the eventful fabrication thought Peter. "May be I will write about the vultures and the carcasses." He said, looking at his dad's picture hung on the wall. You could have thought that it was his dad's room and he was slightly peeking into it. Yes, you are right the room belongs to his dad but Peter inhabits it. He is in the room right now and we are talking about it. The cold steel rail of the railway track seemed to heat in the summer evening and the rust could be smelt in the air. Without the train to pass by and without anybody working on the derailed station the compartments seemed too grassy. The crickets sung their songs every night as the evening folded its way and nature took its course. In the winter the coldness hit the building too. It was warm inside but the cold city in the heat of emptiness numbed the viewer.

Well, to begin a story just like any other post-apocalyptic world would be very untrue and it wouldn't justify the characters inside Peter's head. The city was stuck in time and Peter could still write about it, just the way it was. He could change it but, could he really make it move? He was in a world where the clocks did not move. Things seemed to be stuck where they are, no locomotion and no travelling around. Just a window shaft that could be moved, not the world outside. Peter could move only because he was underground and was not on the surface when the big bang hit the earth. The vultures were in the cave and the dead dog was in the tunnel. They were hidden from the sunshine and the regular moon rise. Only night darkened and the day harkened but nothing could really seem lurking. Peter just did not know who were moving and alive and where everybody was.

Where his dad was? You must have thought that his dad was dead and therefore, his picture was hung on the wall. No, all the moving people had disappeared. Now, the vultures were gone and the carcass was gone. No sign of traces and bits. No remaining minutes could tell what the time was because you never know about the remaining minutes. No any head, nobody living like a vulture or dead likes a carcass could be seen outside. No photographs hung outside. Peter wanted to write about these things. He was devising something; he thought what if for reasons unknown every character disappeared into the unknown.

What would he be creating if he would talk about things which are not in life and do not possess anything lively for that matter? It is just him, and the freaking window. A life that has been turned into a carcass has been eaten by those who could devour it. What would Peter devour? He could not even sustain this story which he has started to write. His dad had left home so that he could earn some money by working in the railway station. Peter had that faint tinge in his mind. He saw the same thing in the outside world. The unmoving railway station and the nature's call which was overlapping the unmoved modern mechanics of the railway which was not enough for a man to feed himself and his lonely child. Man was dependent on the machine here, and the mind of a man saw the machine stuck and unable to cater a need or feed a man, in return. This is what will happen if a man could not move the machine. The time stopped was machine stopped. One thing was sure to happen the nature would engulf it, beneath the green and the vines. Crickets would sound and thrive, Vultures would fill their stomach. The dead would die and the living would live to die.

Stories like this would be thought of being devised but would die in the head of the character that make up the story.

The End

This work blends a mind of an office goer who is trying to find the meaning of life through words of a mystic whom he encounters. How mystic defines the world is important to him. The character is tired with routine, corporate life and wants to end his story.

On a very own sustainable ego, Pal had grown subtly inept to his behaviors. He led a capital life blended with corporate world and media, of the homely shaped colony. He had charities to attend and all the glamour of the ball parties and social grimace consoled him. He hated them. His self of the individual hood was always jointed with the obligations which he shared on his desk or at the boss's office. During presentations and conferences, he was obliged to be brought at the center of the stage. Only to find an excuse in the vulnerable environment he faltered from day-to-day exhortation of the service. He was in a service and that was the only prolonged satisfaction that he got. It was in obligation of the corporate world that he laughed and smiled. It was all very fragile. Just like the homely shaped colony. "You can do anything and be anything in this world, you can do anything you like" said the old mystic to Pal. Therefore, he was there in everything that he could become. Nothing compelled him to not be himself. He was always himself regardless of what people said. He had become one of his kinds.

On a busy day one morning when Pal thought of going to the market he was acquainted with a mystical persona. That person had left family life long ago and his household dwells somewhere else now and resides a far. Mystic, he had become. He was beyond this world. How could he know about the world when he doesn't have to run a livelihood thought Pal? Pal was sometimes curious and anxious enough to think that animals and old aged ones did not have to attend a job. They were free to roam around and do nothing. People, who cooked years and years in the houses, did not need any job. They already had it. Perhaps, Pal was so overwhelmed with the question of mystic beholding affairs of the world.

Pal had only few answers which he used for his day to day affairs. On a bus ride he would ask the driver to stop on a particular road or gully. Actually, the driver always knew Pal due to his frequent travels on the same route. The difference between the mystic and himself is what he realized when he knew that to become a mystic one had to renounce what one has had possessed to his/her credit. Have no grudges with life or no mysteries in life cooking on the other side of the story. Maybe renouncing what one had is attaining a mystic state of mind.

Pal knew that the mystic could answer every questions raised by the world, but he wouldn't answer in terms of the world. There would be no world in some of his answers. The mystic did not answer for the world to solve every issue. He ignored some aspects of the worldly answers. There is no inspection into that further by the great mystic. Pal had also believed in the mysterious recognition of myth. The aims of such work were to console and grip the belief of invulnerability.

Those who were consoled by day to day affairs did not seek god or Supreme Being. Pal felt out of this world when he couldn't connect the dots. Just then he would realize that he had seen the mystic through his eyes and the mystic was like him, unlike his appearances. The mystic looked like him. He looked so worldly to Pal that the world he inhibited was very lethal and observant. For the dying ones, the world existed in death and for the alive, in life of day to day reality. The world was not seized by the mystic in some way. He also lived there and tried to decipher. Others are not prone to mysticism. It is also stepping beyond this world. For Pal he was in this world, in terms of business, money, employment, prices of the goods and also love. "Another being is required for love", said Pal. "Being, like my being" he used to say on his lunch hour to the staff of corporate house where Pal worked. He dealt with media and advertising clients. His job was to decipher too. However, unlike the mystic and the 'ism' Pal was perplexed with his job technologically. Technically, he did what he could and thought he existed for others in that sense. But they only appreciated the ends and not the process. His labor was not seen in designing cards for his clients. His research of the market was not compared to his ability to perceive and know the society. Pal also did calculations. And only importance was the end of the work waiting to be completed and done. So, Pal has moved to the end now. He wanted his story to become an end.

Unlike many other ending, Pal wanted me to end the story. I being the narrator and narrating an end. What happened to Pal will be a question to public appraisals. Pal suffocates with the idea of the social. Showing a politically correct but politically flawed aspect of the story I repose to solitude. I want the character to become unsocial and in mere terms a psychopath who has been turned into one by the society. When his ends did not meet he became an end product of the society. So, Pal wanted to end his story. I end it with his character. His self is under the disguise and hence an end is on par with the character. Maybe he should relocate himself and reside with his new self and new identity, and live another life with it. But it would be a same thing for another life, with other rules and again another end, but the character, same.

Knockings on the Door

Deepak was playing with his old lighter. His old room had just got a new friend. The old typist was overjoyed and was not sad at all when Deepak bought a new typewriter for his room from the typist. Deepak would write every morning and would try to immerse in it. Deepak sometimes wrote poetry, but he was striving for some short fiction. Like a crispy taste of a potato chip, crispy words from Deepak's mouth dropped like an atom bomb, and blasted all over the pages. All by himself, Deepak would hear the ticking of the wall clock and the wall lizard. He slightly philosophized their ticking and thought about it. He had read the morning news that day and had come to know that the English broadsheet had announced a story writing competition with a huge amount of cash prize. Deepak had a compulsion to get the prize. His landlord had threatened him for the rent. The landlord was away for now but was returning any day soon. Deepak needed to hurry.

Deepak shaved and got ready to write something, he had carefully parted hair, a fair complexion which the shaving enlightened more, he was tall and slim. In the morning light he was still wearing a nightdress and he looked like a blown-out candle withstanding the wind. He was swift in his appearance. He would immerse in his chair beside the window, which faced the pond. Deepak would sometimes visit the pond and would write poetry. "I lost the tide in my heart/ Looking at a ripple in my pond." This was what Deepak once wrote. For him the tide was the story which he hadn't begun yet.

Deepak thought hurriedly in his thoughts and movements, he was walking restlessly inside his room from one corner to another. "Landlord would return any day; I should finish the story and send it to the broadsheet before the deadline is over." Deepak's room was above the cacophony of the city, tourist guides would come and go, they would give a wailing cry to the tourists and take them to their destinations. Surya was a tourist guide who worked night shift, and would stand below Deepak's room. The wailing in the concrete was like a chilled air of winter, which touched everyone. Overlooking a window Deepak was all set for writing. His landlord who had gone to the village to take care of his sick mother would be coming anytime now. It was difficult for Deepak to take care of his writing because of the quick deadline and the overwhelming pressure about the landlord. The wailing road and the bustle of the city distracted him this time. It was already night now, and Deepak was not able to decide a title for his work. He remembered his student days in Delhi when he would write a research paper first and then would decide the title later. It worked somehow.

"I have to solve three problems; write a story before the deadline extinguishes, arrange money for the landlord if I am unable to get my writing published and decide my title." Triviality of these issues haunted Deepak. The only good thing happening was at the backdrop of the window. The city welcomed tourists and after all, it was modern Kathmandu. All the money that Deepak had was gone; he had bought a typewriter with it. He did it for sheer interest. He thought he can approach the old typist and borrow some money, but he couldn't approach him as he lacked courage. The next day Deepak woke up with a knock on his door. He peeped through the peephole and found that it was Surya, the tourist guide.

"Good morning, my man. How well are you living today?"

"Came by to see you, saw your curtains closed for this warm sunlight of winter."

Surya talked through the peephole and Deepak opened the door to let him in.

Deepak said "Good morning. I was disturbed by the city yesterday, so the curtain is still closed."

"How did your night shift go?"

"As usual" replied Surya. "Nothing new is happening; tourists still visit us, as long as they keep coming business keep shape."

"Something external has to knock our door so we can open up, you know." Deepak seemed to find the guide meaningful.

It reflected Deepak's situation. What would be his external factor that would knock his door?"

In the meanwhile there was another knock on the door

"Open up, I have a business with you, Mister." The landlord shouted behind the door.

It was a fine morning, but it was getting darker for Deepak. The landlord was already here and perhaps would ask for the money, he hadn't written a story and there was no question to think about the unwritten title, unlike those student days in Delhi. Deepak thought to face it all, and he opened the door.

"My mother in the village passed away; I performed her funeral rites yesterday," said the landlord.

Deepak felt sorry for the landlord and he also realized that the landlord is not in need of the money at this immediate hour because the landlord actually needed the money for his mother's medicine. Deepak began to inquire the landlord about the funeral rites and he managed to get hold of some information which he thought might be meaningful for his story which he was about to begin. He also talked about the experiences of the tourist guide, and asked how foreigners react or what do they share when they visit the country. Differences in funeral rites in Kathmandu and other cities of the world also became one of his diverse topics.

By the evening a manuscript was ready, the two knockings on the door helped Deepak to write a story and finish it, and it was all ready to be sent for the broadsheet. After two days Deepak got a letter that the story was accepted and it won the competition. Deepak's narration, experiences, and the philosophy of the external factors knocking on the door paved its way to success.

Deepak fictionalized the reality well. All those information were real, and they only needed to be fictionalized. Any sudden reality could come like a shock in our life and perhaps we should learn to fictionalize it, and suit it to ourselves. We just need to open the door and face the problems. The case could have been different for Deepak if the landlord's mother hadn't passed away. However, that is not the case and the reality can never be understood beforehand; such is the slipping fate of a human. The case for Deepak made him a good observer and a great deal of his patience was put under test.

About the Author

Sushant Thapa

Sushant Thapa (born on 26 February 1993) is an award-winning Nepalese poet from Biratnagar-13, Nepal, who holds an M.A. in English literature from Jawaharlal Nehru University (JNU) in New Delhi, India.

He has published seven books of English poetry, namely: The Poetic Burden and Other Poems (Authorspress, New Delhi, 2020), Abstraction and Other Poems (Impspired, UK, 2021), Minutes of Merit (Haoajan, Kolkata, 2021), Love's Cradle (World Inkers Printing and Publishing, New York, USA and Senegal, Africa, 2023), Spontaneity: A New Name of Rhyme (Ambar Publication House, New Delhi, 2023), Chorus of Simplicity and Other New Poems (Ukiyoto Publishing, 2024) and Finding My Soul in Kathmandu (Ukiyoto Publishing, 2024). "The One Rupee Taker and Other Stories from Nepal" is his first collection of flash fiction and short stories. He works as an English lecturer in Biratnagar, Nepal, and as an assistant editor of Himalaya Diary, an online portal.

Milton Keynes UK
Ingram Content Group UK Ltd.
UKHW031634201124
451457UK00006B/61